MW00909618

It's *ALMOST* My Birthday.

Written and Illustrated by Shelly Emery

It's *ALMOST* My Birthday.

Summary: A young boy takes us through the months
of the year as he plans and anxiously awaits his birthday.

ISBN 978-1479120017

There is nothing more exciting to a child than a birthday, and when you are five years old *everyday* is ***ALMOST*** your birthday!

To all the children who have passed through the doors of my classroom,

you are the ones that have taught me to celebrate everyday as my ***ALMOST*** birthday.

May you never lose that excitement for life.

~ *Miss Emery*

It's *almost* my Birthday.
I can hardly wait.

Calendar
January
February
March
May
June
September
November
December

Everyone's invited.
You better not be late!

March
S M T W T F S
26 27 28 29 30 31
ROCK
PAUL
PAUL
MOM
PAUL
Mikey
Vince
Gina
CHRIS
Katie
Blaise
Me
PARTY LIST
STREAMERS
BALLOONS
CAKE
GAMES
HATS
YOU'RE INVITED

We will wear our party hats
and mine will be the best

because my birthday is my special day
where I’m the honored guest!

A clown will make us animals
from colorful balloons.

We'll dance and march around the room
to happy birthday tunes!

It’s *almost* my birthday.
I know my friends will all be there.

We will have an awesome time.
Nothing can compare!

We'll play pin the tail on the donkey.
Everyone will get a spin,
and since it is my birthday
I am sure that I will win!

It's *almost* my birthday.
It's time to celebrate....

all the things that make me special,
all the things that make me great!

We will all eat birthday cake
and ice cream in a dish.

I will blow the candles out
and make a special wish.

It's *almost* my birthday.
My special day is almost here.

It's the most important day.
I plan for it all year.

June
S M T W T F S
KNOEBELS
PAUL
PAUL
PAUL
PAUL
TO DO:
Pick cake
Send invites
Get Balloons
call Clown
Games
CLOWN
275-0563
Candy
PARTY HATS

My friends will bring me presents
and treat me like a king.

Everyone will be so happy.
I bet that they will sing!

We'll break a colorful piñata
and watch the candy fall,
and because it is my birthday
I bet I catch the most of all!

I’ll hang so many decorations,
balloons and streamers too.
Throw some colorful confetti
in red and green and blue.

Today it was my birthday.
We partied all day long!
Happy Birthday

We ate some cake, we played some games and sang the birthday song!

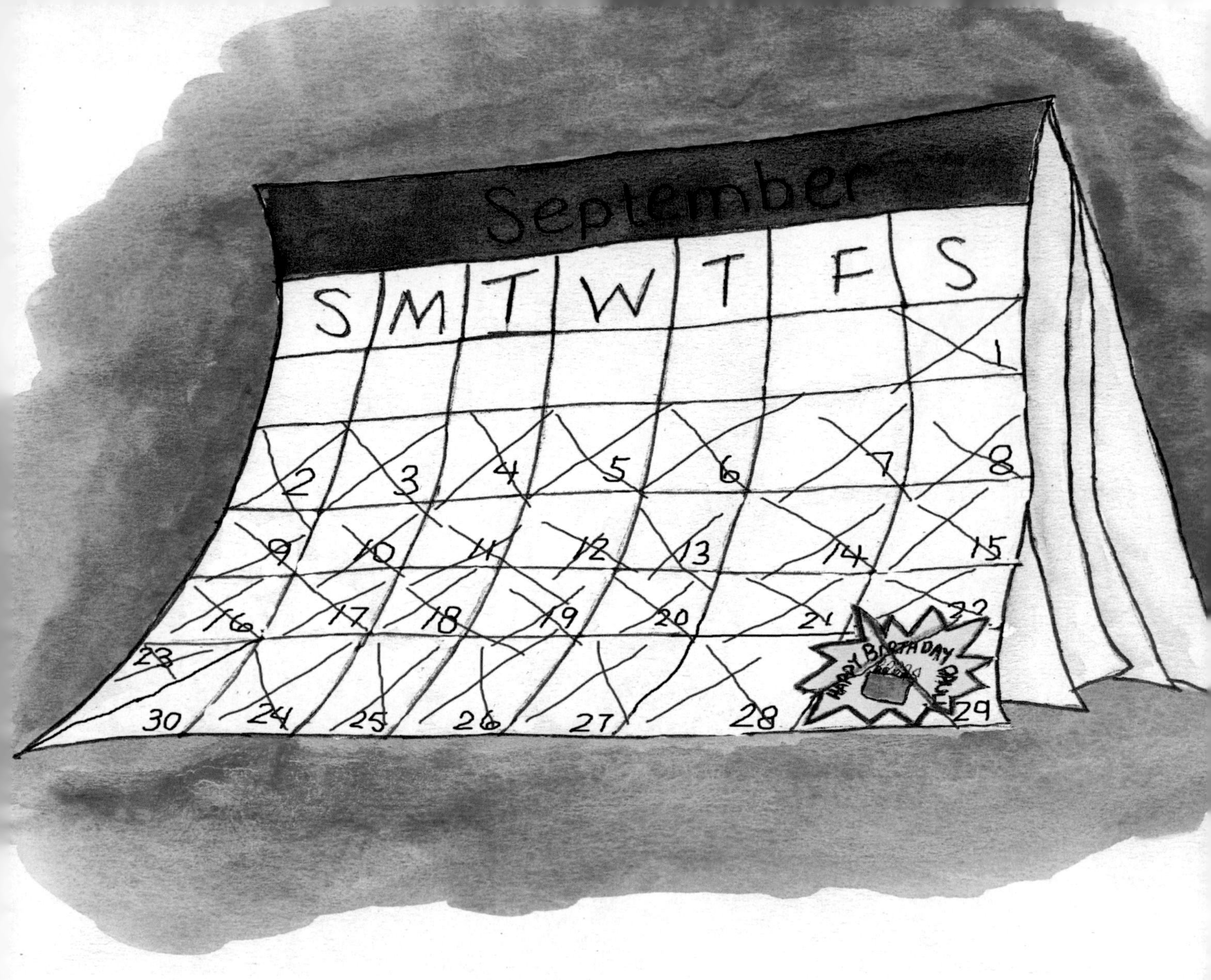

Now my birthday's over.
It's time to go to bed.
Sleeping on my pillow,
I'll dream of my birthday in my head.

Because........

Happy Birthday Paul!

It’s *almost* my birthday.
It will soon be here!
It will be here before you know it.

It only takes a year!

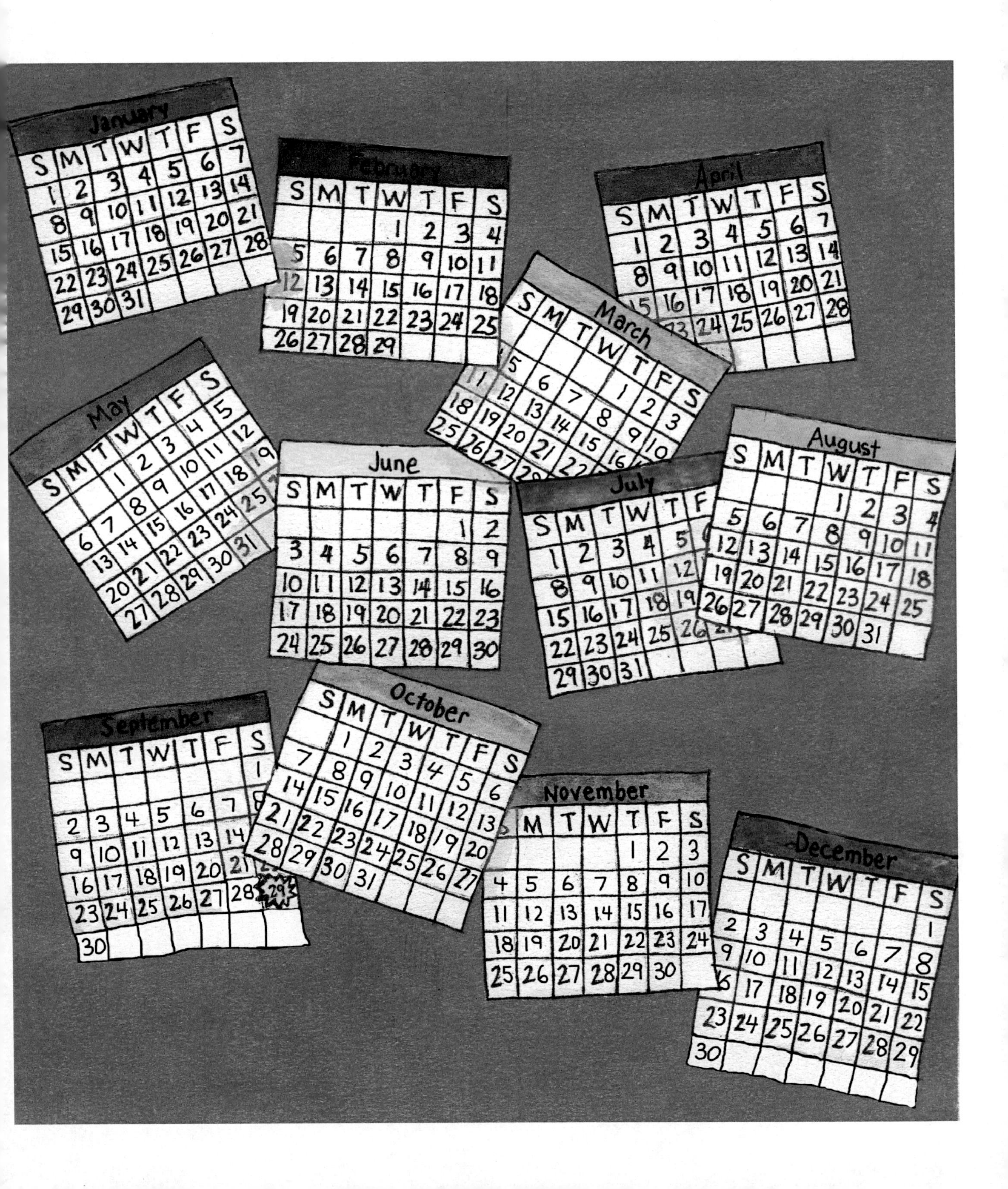

About the Author:

Shelly Emery currently resides in Danville, PA, where she has been a preschool teacher since 2001.
She studied at the Ringling School of Art and Design in Sarasota, FL, in 1992. Shelly graduated from Kutztown University with a B.S. degree in Elementary Education.
She is currently pursuing her Master's in Illustration at Hollins University in Roanoke, VA.